There Was an Old Lady Who Swallowed a Bat!

by Lucille Colandro
Illustrated by Jared Lee

SCHOLASTIC INC.

Cartwheel
B·O·O·K·S®

New York   Toronto   London   Auckland   Sydney
Mexico City   New Delhi   Hong Kong   Buenos Aires

To my favorite wizards — David and Gene
Love,
L.C.

To my daughter Jana
who loves Halloween
— J.L.

No part of this publication may be reproduced, stored in a retrieval system, or transmitted in
any form or by any means, electronic, mechanical, photocopying, recording, or otherwise,
without written permission of the publisher. For information regarding permission, write to
Scholastic Inc., Attention: Permissions Department, 557 Broadway, New York, NY 10012.

ISBN-13: 978-0-439-82791-1
ISBN-10: 0-439-82791-4

Text copyright © 2002 by Lucille Santarelli. Illustrations copyright © 2002 by Jared Lee.
All rights reserved. Published by Scholastic Inc. SCHOLASTIC, CARTWHEEL BOOKS,
and associated logos are trademarks and/or registered trademarks of Scholastic Inc.

36 35   18 19/0

Printed in the U.S.A.   40

This edition first printing, September 2006

There was an old lady
who swallowed a bat.
I don't know why she swallowed a bat,
imagine that.

There was an old lady
who swallowed an owl.

My, oh, my, she started to howl.

She swallowed the owl to shush the bat.
I don't know why she swallowed a bat,
imagine that.

There was an old lady
who swallowed a cat.
What do you think? Now she's so fat.

She swallowed the cat to chase the owl.

She swallowed the owl to shush the bat.
I don't know why she swallowed a bat,
imagine that.

There was an old lady
who swallowed a ghost.
What do you think?

She liked it the most!

She swallowed the ghost to catch the cat.
She swallowed the cat to chase the owl.

She swallowed the owl to shush the bat.
I don't know why she swallowed a bat,
imagine that.

There was an old lady
who swallowed a goblin.

It made her so dizzy, she started to spin.

She swallowed the goblin

to scare the ghost.

She swallowed the ghost to catch the cat.

She swallowed the cat to chase the owl.

She swallowed the owl to shush the bat.
I don't know why she swallowed a bat,
imagine that.

There was an old lady
who swallowed some bones.

There were so many, she started to groan.

She swallowed the bones to rattle the goblin.

She swallowed the goblin to scare the ghost.

She swallowed the ghost to catch the cat.

She swallowed the cat to chase the owl.
She swallowed the owl to shush the bat.

I don't know why she swallowed a bat,
imagine that.

There was an old lady
who swallowed a wizard

to cast a spell so she could yell,

"TRICK OR

TREAT!"